Star Girl Saves the Concert

Jill McDougall
Illustrated by Pedro J Colombo

The children were at school.
They were going to have a concert.

Sneaky Pete was cross.
“I do not like the noise,” he said.
“I will stop the concert.”
BANG!
BANG!

The children walked out of the hall.

Sneaky Pete took the big drum.
"That will stop the concert," he said.
HA! HA!

“Who will help us?” said the children.
“I will help you!” said Star Girl.

Sneaky Pete jumped in his boat and drove off.
"I will stop you, Sneaky Pete," said Star Girl.

Star Girl sent out a big hook on a rope.

Star Girl got Sneaky Pete.
“BRMM! BRMM!” went the boat.
The boat could not go!

Sneaky Pete cut the rope.

Sneaky Pete drove off.
"Ha, ha!" he said.
"You can't get me now!"

Star Girl sent out a big net.

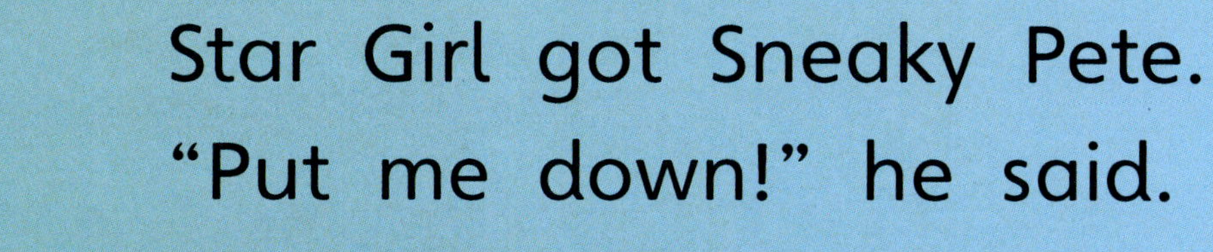

Star Girl got Sneaky Pete.
"Put me down!" he said.

Star Girl took Sneaky Pete back to the school.

“Thank you Star Girl!” said the children. “Now we can have the concert.”

Star Girl made Sneaky Pete help, too.